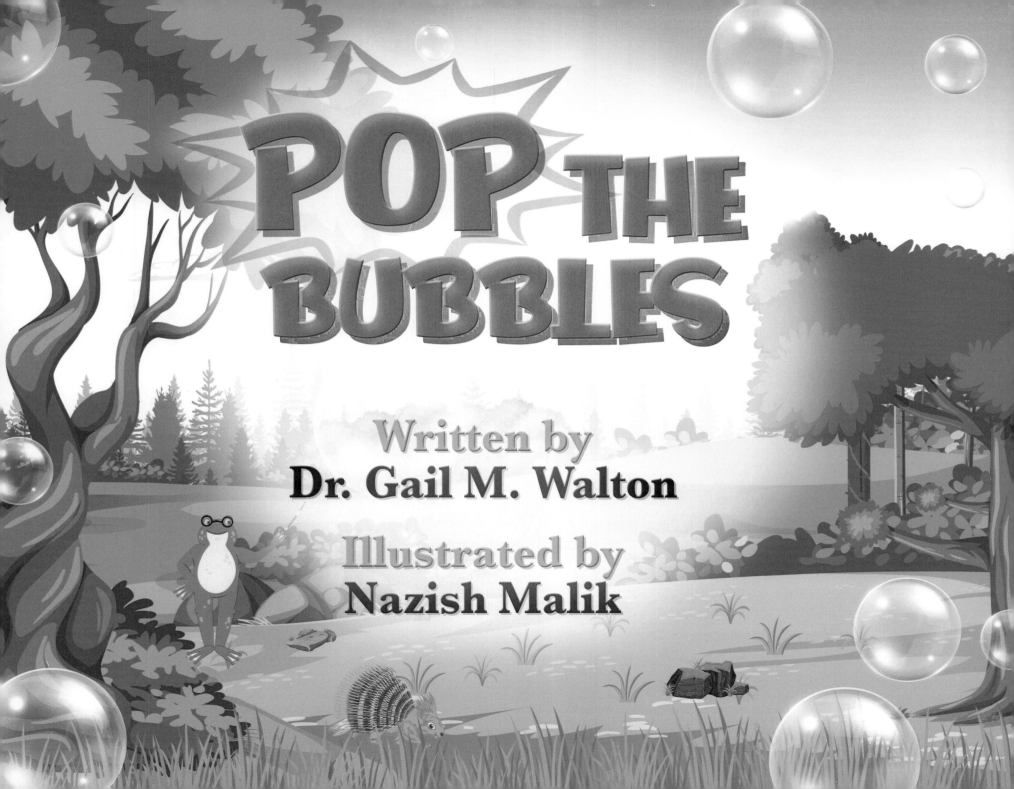

# POP THE BUBBLES

Written by
## Dr. Gail M. Walton

Illustrated by
## Nazish Malik

Paperback ISBN: 979-8-9851812-0-3
Hardback ISBN: 979-8-9851812-1-0
Library of Congress Control Number:  2021922438

PRINTED IN THE UNITED STATES OF AMERICA

**MELVON**

1233 The Plaza #5175
Charlotte, NC 28299

www.themelvonco.com
executive@themelvonco.com
(980) 288-8608

Facebook: https://www.facebook.com/TheMelvonCo
Instagram: https://www.instagram.com/themelvonco/
Facebook: https://www.facebook.com/DrGailMWalton
Instagram:  https://www.instagram.com/drgailmwalton/

Tervon,

Thank you for showing me
what true love is.
Yo te amo!

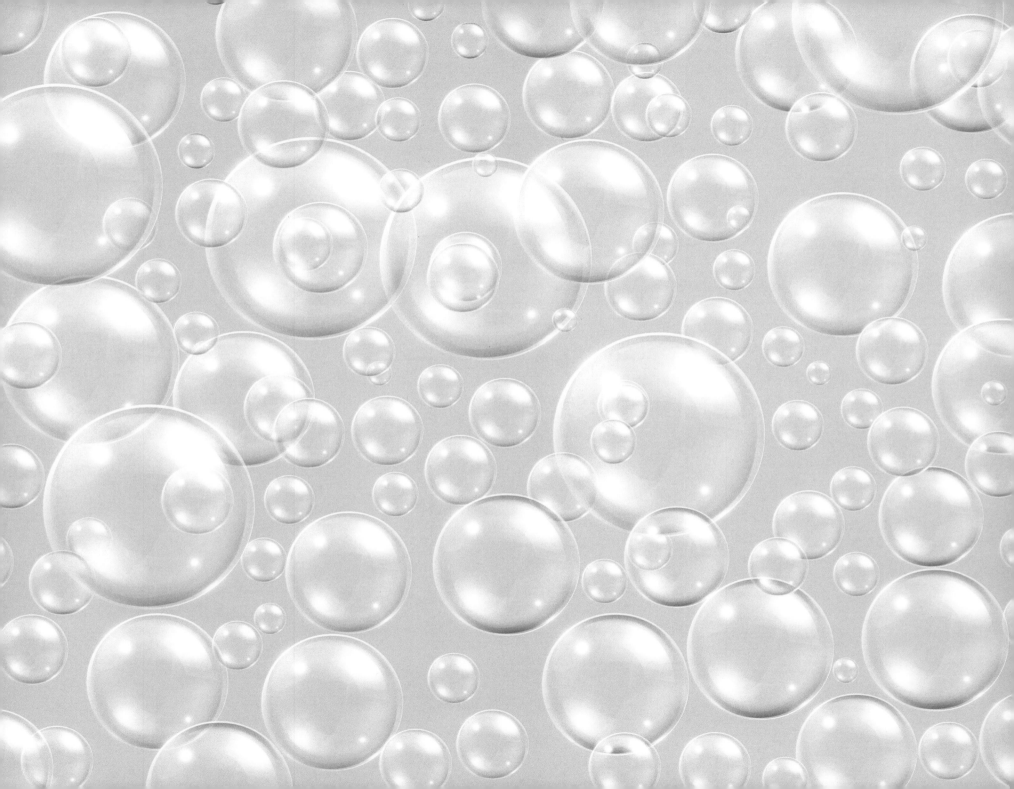

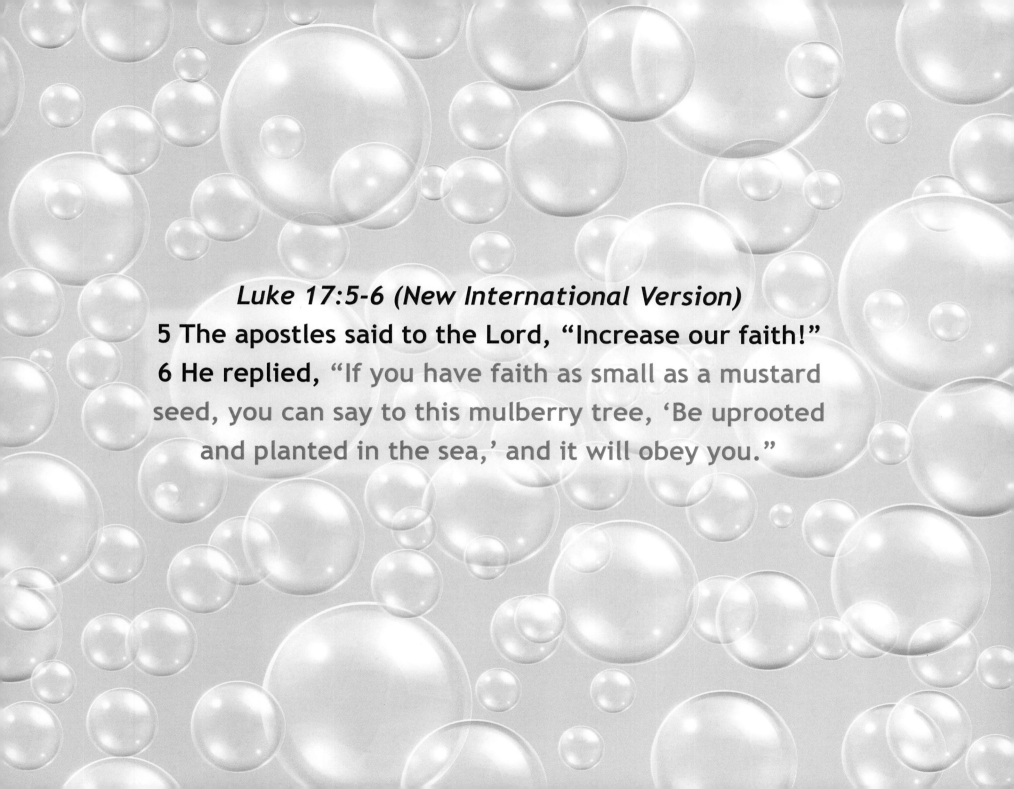

*Luke 17:5-6 (New International Version)*

**5 The apostles said to the Lord, "Increase our faith!"**

**6 He replied,** "If you have faith as small as a mustard seed, you can say to this mulberry tree, 'Be uprooted and planted in the sea,' and it will obey you."

As I go walking, I look at all the beautiful things around me.

Hey, what's that up ahead? I have
never seen flowers like that before.

The flowers float in the air all around. Some of my friends smell the new flowers.

Oh no, my friends are turning blue! They are getting sick.

It looks like they have a fever.

They are sneezing and coughing. I am worried about them.

I need to do something.
Who should I ask for help?

I know! I will ask Mr. Green. He will know what to do.

"Mr. Green, my friends smelled the red flowers and now they are all sick. Can you help them?"

"Yes, I can. I will have to swim to the bottom of the pond and find the magic seeds that will make them better."

"But first, I will blow a bubble and put you in it to keep you safe. Ribbit."

Mr. Green also blows bubbles for the rest of my friends who have not smelled the flowers. We float around in the forest. The bubbles protect us from getting sick.

We eat inside our bubbles.

We sleep inside our bubbles.

We even play inside our bubbles.
I am bored inside my bubble.

Mr. Green swims deep down into the pond to find the magic seeds. He searches everywhere but cannot find them. He searches underneath a shell.

He looks behind a large rock.

He even peeks around the plants, but he still
does not find them. He is ready to give up.

Mr. Green sits on a tree stump and asks, "Where can they be?"

Then he looks down and notices that his feet are touching the seeds inside the tree stump. He has found the magic seeds!

Mr. Green gives each of my sick friends a seed and then sprinkles some over the field of red flowers. The flowers disappear.

At last, my friends are all feeling better now.
We don't need to be in our bubbles anymore.

Lightning Source UK Ltd.
Milton Keynes UK
UKRC031205100322
399867UK00001B/6

* 9 7 9 8 9 8 5 1 8 1 2 1 0 *